nickelodeon.

DORA the EXPLORER™

I Love My Papi!

By Alison Inches

Illustrated by Dave Aikins

Random House 🏠 New York

Hi! I'm Dora.

I love to spend time
with my papi.

Papi teaches me
a soccer kick.

I kick the ball.
Goal!

When we play baseball,
Papi coaches my team.

I swing the bat.
I slide into home!

On weekends,

Papi and I ride bikes.

Or we sail
on a boat.

In the summer,
we go
to the beach.

We build
sand castles.
We play
in the waves!

Papi is a good cook.

We bake a cake.

Yum! Yum!

Sometimes we pack
a picnic.
We share it
with Boots.

Papi can build
anything.

He makes us
a tire swing!

For a treat,
Papi takes us
to the circus.
Boots loves the clowns.

Every night,
Papi tucks me
into bed.

Then we read
a book.
I like books
about animals.

I love my <u>papi</u>!
And my <u>papi</u> loves me.